RiSiNG
STARS
NEW
YOUNG
pVOICES iN
POETRY

Acknowledgements

With grateful thanks to the following people for their
invaluable assistance, mentoring and advice:

Joelle Taylor, poet, Artistic Director of the Poetry Society's
national youth slam championships, SLAMbassadors,
and coach of the national team

Ian Dodds, Deputy Programme Leader, Illustration,
School of Visual Communication, Birmingham City University

Franziska Liebig, Company Manager, Pop Up Projects

Special thanks to Arts Council England for supporting
Rising Stars through their Grants for the Arts

Text copyright © 2017 Ruth Awololo, Victoria Adukwei Bulley,
Abigail Cook, Jay Hulme, Amina Jama
Illustrations copyright © 2017 Riya Chowdhury, Elanor Chuah, Joe Manners

Cover design by Arianna Osti

First published in Great Britain and in the USA in 2017 by
Otter-Barry Books, Little Orchard, Burley Gate, Herefordshire, HR1 3QS
www.otterbarrybooks.com

A catalogue record for this book is available from the British Library.

ISBN 978-1-910959-37-4

Printed in Great Britain

9 8 7 6 5 4 3 2 1

Rising Stars: New Young Voices in Poetry

Poems by
RUTH AWOLOLA ★ VICTORIA ADUKWEI BULLEY
ABIGAIL COOK ★ JAY HULME ★ AMINA JAMA

Illustrations by
RIYA CHOWDHURY, ELANOR CHUAH, JOE MANNERS

Otter-Barry BOOKS

CONTENTS

ABIGAIL COOK poems

JAY HULME poems

AMINA JAMA poems

Introduction

Rising Stars is a showcase of – and a platform for – some of the most brilliant emerging young poets writing today. We can't pretend to have discovered them; with the help of Joelle Taylor, founder and director of SLAMbassadors, Pop Up and Otter-Barry Books tapped into the UK's spoken word community, where we wanted to find writer-performers interested in making the journey into poetry for young readers.

We most certainly found what we were looking for!

There are myriad universes in this dazzling collection of new poems by Ruth, Victoria, Abigail, Jay and Amina, who are the 'rising stars' of its title. These are the thrilling voices of young writers on the brink of discovery, exploring their own inner worlds while contemplating the vastness of the cosmos: Ruth has "witnessed creation" and "stuffs universes into pockets", Abigail declares "I am constellations" and Jay takes notice of "the universe held within my soul".

Poetry surges like a force of nature through their veins, making poems as powerful as songs and spells, infused with wonder and magic. Abigail "weaved stories into the silences" while Ruth sings of "wild souls, captured" inside her. Jay finds "one thousand languages" with which to "speak to new people" and forge a "fully formed community". Victoria feels the weight of poetry – "the poet's pen is heavy" – but wields it defiantly in the brilliant 'This Poem Is Not About Parakeets'. Amina paints with her words – "she wore blue better than a sunset wore orange" – intimate, lyrical impressions and memories of family, places, prayers and dreams.

Whatever it is you discover in this eloquent collection, have no doubt that between these pages you'll encounter some of the brightest lights in poetry today – alongside outstanding first-time illustrators from Birmingham City University, Riya Chowdhury, Elanor Chuah and Joe Manners.

Truly, these are the stars to watch out for.

Dylan Calder, Director, Pop Up Projects

RUTH AWOLOLA

Illustrations by Joe Manners

Mainly About Aliens

I'm looking up into the sky
And I am thinking, how can it be this big?
Why is there so much of it?
How do we all fit?
I am thinking all these things
But I am mainly thinking about aliens.

Wondering whether there is someone or something
Doing the same.
Looking up,
Hoping or knowing there is life out there.

I wonder if we'd welcome the aliens,
Respect their alien ways,
Watch when they show us new colours,
Listen when they talk about their part of the sky.
I wonder if they'll say, "We come in peace,"
If they'll even have a word for peace on their planet.
Maybe they don't have guns
Or war,
Or maybe they are running away from it.

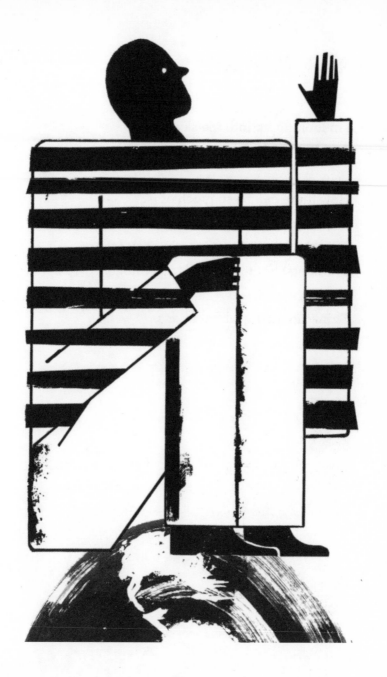

I'm looking up into the sky
And I'm thinking, why is it so big?

How there can be so much of it?
If we can all fit?
Thinking about how we treat each other,
Thinking about how we'd treat aliens,

Thinking mainly about aliens.

Superpowers

My little brother loves superheroes.
He wants to change the world,
get the keys to the city and save the girl.

I watch the films with him all the time,
whenever he is sad,
whenever he really wants our mum or dad.

When we're late to school
and we're running down the street,
I tell him he's the fastest man that I'll ever meet.

And I can't deny he's strong,
with all he has to do,
though he's yet to master the art of Jujutsu.

Our parents must think we're clever,
they let us do everything on our own:
cook, clean and take care of the home.

I think we might have powers,
the ones that are most believable.
I think to our parents
we might be invisible.

A Love Letter to the Stars

I have always wanted to be nocturnal,
To live by the light of the moon.
There's something about the stars – they're eternal.
I pray the sun sets soon.

Dreams and wishes and hope and light,
Placed perfectly in the sky.
I'll never understand the power of the night,
How it fills me with love or why?

There are things I hate about space,
It's far too big and unknown.
But it is my safe place,
I long to call it home.

I'm in love with the stars,
how they are mine and ours.

Wolves

We are staring at the moon
and I think for a second we become
wolves again.
Screaming at the stars,
growling at the idea
that this night might end
and we will forget this moment,
as in turn we will be forgotten.
Our wild souls
captured.

We become wolves,
and for once we are running for something.
Instead of running from it.

On Forgetting That I Am a Tree

A poem in which I am growing.

A poem in which I am a tree,
And I am both appreciated and undervalued.

A poem in which I fear I did not dig into the past,
Did not think about my roots,
Forgot what it meant to be planted.

A poem in which I realise they may try to cut
    me down,
That I must change with the seasons,
That I do it so well
It looks as if they are changing with me.

A poem in which I remember I have existed
    for centuries,
That centuries are far too small a unit of
    measurement,
That time found itself in the forests, woods
    and jungles.
Remember I have witnessed creation,
That I am key to it.

A poem in which some will carve their names
    into my skin
In hopes the universe will know them.
Where I am so tall I kiss the sun.
Trees cannot hide,
They belong to the day and to the night,
To the past and the future.

A poem in which I stop looking for it,
Because I am home.
I am habitat.
My branches are host and shelter.
I am life-giver and fruit-bearer.
Self-sufficient protection.

A poem in which I remember I am a tree.

Ta, Love

There's something of the rich tea biscuits dipped
    in a sugary brew,
From the inside it warms you up.
Something of the feeling ever so welcome
When Dylan's mom says,
"Ta, Love."

Pockets

Her pockets are never empty.
She says pockets are for running.
So she keeps them full,
Stuffs universes into them,
And says it is just the essentials.

She says: if we get stranded,
If aliens take us,
If there's an apocalypse,
There will be no time for bags.

She treats pockets
Like built-in spaces for hope.
Lets the weight of it
Pull down her baggy trousers.

Readies herself for any eventuality,
Revels in her own lack of normality.

A Love That is Baking

We share accidental glances
as if they are a:
fresh out of the oven,
warm to touch,
soft in the middle,
just right on the outside
loaf of bread.
Pulled apart by a baker's hands.
Not exactly equal,
but with good intentions.

There is something so sweet
about a love that is baking.

Rising with the heat.

VICTORIA ADUKWEI BULLEY

Illustrations by Riya Chowdhury

Auntie Lucille

after Lucille Clifton

Auntie Lucille was born with
six fingers on each hand.
This, she wrote, went back through all
the women in her bloodline, all the way
across the sea, to Dahomey – a place
which isn't called that any more.

Not that I've ever been there,
or known Lucille myself.
She's not my mum's sister, not even
Mum's friend – just Auntie Lucille
who smiles from the cover of her book,
a patron saint of black girls anywhere,
a healer of history with soft words.

Any poet's pen is heavy, some say
it takes two hands to hold one.
Weighed down by countless stories,
it's a wonder that a writer writes at all, when
words fail or escape, facts become myths,
or worse, forgotten. Still, if anyone could tell
how to carry the past in one piece, Auntie Lucille,
with twelve fingers, would know.

Toby Killed the Bird

Toby killed the bird at first light,
left the hallway dashed with feathers:
a fraction of a pillow fight.

Before we woke up, after night,
and hoovered up the snowy weather,
Toby killed the bird at first light.

He must have heard it screech in flight,
its tiny frame (though made for measure),
a fraction of a pillow fight.

No small thing would keep its life
in needle jaws closed tight together.
Toby killed the bird at first light

and who am I to say what's right
when my kind kill for fur and leisure?
A fraction of a pillow fight –

one way to say what it looked like
when wild prey met tame predator.
Toby killed the bird at first light.
A fraction of a pillow fight.

Afro Hair Haiku

My hair shrinks when wet,
like pine cones in the autumn
waiting for their time.

Here's one thing I love:
to curl it round my fingers
and watch it bounce back.

Sometimes I wear braids.
Other times I wear cornrows.
Any style looks good.

I used to harm it,
force it down, flat and lifeless –
a ghost of itself.

Now I let it grow
the way it wants to grow:
confident again.

How to Build a Kitchen

Toast jumping?
a flight into space

and butter melting?
the tide going low

and tea brewing?
night sky before storms

and cakes baking?
our car during summer

and beans soaking?
pebbles in the sea

and eggs boiling?
an invitation to crack

and tomatoes blended?
the first red paint

and onions golden?
    the start of any stew

and mushrooms frying?
    a sign of Sunday

and ground chilli falling?
    like red hot rain

and bread rising?
    the sun on hills

the smell as it rises?
    the last dream before dawn

This Poem Is Not About Parakeets

On the bus back, two men make noise and all else
falls silent, or leans away. One woman gets off
altogether. I pull my headphones out. The air
thickens. The men are angry. Words leave their
mouths and hit the windows like flies. *They're
everywhere, everywhere you look.* I've got seven
stops left. *What we want is our country back.*
My armpits tingle with sweat. I want to throw
something and then leave. *Is that so much to ask?*
I'm nowhere near home, so instead I think about the
parakeets that live on my road. *They take up all the
housing.* I want to tell the men how the parakeets
got here. *All they do is take our jobs.* How they
were brought here in the '60s for a film, and then
escaped. *They're scroungers.* I want to tell them
how despite the bad weather they never lost their
songs. *Why are they so noisy?* How none of April's
showers ever washed their colours off. *They don't
even try to blend in.* Or how these birds are so smart

they can talk human. *They don't even speak proper English.* The men keep moaning. *It's my freedom of speech.* I want to ask if they've seen these creatures fly, these emerald green parakeets that live near my home, I want to tell them about the brightest, most beautiful birds I've ever known.

Hate

Chew it for long enough
and it'll change taste,

take on a sweetness
that makes you forget to eat,

leaving you starved
of life and love.

Love

Your heart beating
      (without permission)

Your lungs breathing like clockwork
      (without ever having been asked)

Your body working
      (without a thought –
            without ever having demanded love
            back from you)

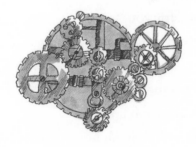

Strange Dusts

In the city today, you see
how the lungs of a desert
some thousand miles away
exhale strange dusts
as far afield as here.

The free papers it carries
will call it
foreign – this air
African, dry, oddly warm
does not belong –
pollution, on the news.
Beautiful
but bad for you.
Holy and hazardous

and now the car you woke to
needs washing again:
its gunmetal finish now
shrouded in sand.

This is the work
of the gentle laugh
of the desert,
languorous
and light.

To Yashika, leaving the city
against your will, do not forget:
air is indiscriminate
and wind knows
no such thing
as nations.

ABIGAIL COOK

Illustrations by Riya Chowdhury

My Body

My body is the garden I grew up in,
with tree-trunk legs,
lungs made of rose bushes.
My ribs are a bird cage,
my skin has a sunflower glow.
I have planted vines that wrap up my arms and
around my thighs.
One day I will teach my children to climb them.

My hair is the ocean,
every curl another wave
to hit the shore of my neck,
every freckle a star in the galaxy.
I am constellations.

My shoulders are bird's wings,
my eyes pearls found in a sea of storms.
My stretchmarks are lightning bolts
that show I can survive growth.

My body is the garden I grew up in.
Every day I walk through it,
marvel at my petal eyelids,
the mountain of my back,
the clouds of my stomach.
I am learning to let my garden grow.
I am learning
to love
every snail,
every stone,
every blossom,
for this is everything
that I am.

Brother

He smells like home
a lingering, familiar smell
that reminds me of long summer memories
stretched like the horizon
for days.

One night
we lay on the driveway
and counted every star
in the sky
plucked them and placed them in our pockets
there to light the way for the darkness ahead
the one that sat in the corners of our bedrooms
and came out of the mouths of the people we loved.

We weaved stories into the silences.
He made me brave.

Hope

I fell down a rabbit hole once,
darkness seeped into the cracks of my skin.
I never believed
I would see the sun again.
But her smile
and his laugh
told me I was wrong.

Night-time in the Garden

Teardrop pearls,
petal eyelids.
Daisies stain the cheeks.

Little girls in nightdresses
run around the garden
singing *A ring a ring o' roses.*

This is snow-globe stillness.

We sit under a toadstool
and count petals on sunflowers.
"She loves me; she loves me not."

We wash ourselves in raindrops,
sleep covered in leaves,
count every star in the sky,
watch the world go by.

Tsunamis fall from the fireplace in the living room.

Rise

And when they try
to clip your wings,
tell you
to sit down, shut up:
rise.

When they tell you
you are too much this way
and too little that way:
rise.

Remember you are falcon bones
and phoenix wings,
so fly.

You are worthy.

Storm of a Girl

I have two storms inside me
I call them my mother and father.

I have my mother's eyes
blue like oceans
like skies on hot summer days.

I have my father's hands
they hold worlds inside them
one day they taught me of planets and galaxies.

Together
I am a hurricane.

You Are the Ocean

You, with your shy smile
and batting eyes.

You, with fists clenched
around your heart.

You, who never learnt
to fit in.

You are everything,
you are waves
and tides
and ferocious.

You are the ocean.

Summer Day

The summer was long and hot.
We sat outside in our pyjamas
whilst the world ended.
It smelt of the perfume my mother wore, and pizza.
My brother and I
made the roundabout our home,
created a roof out of the tree,
made a carpet from the grass,
daisies littering the floor all scattered and dewy.

We drank lemonade
and stayed away from houses with mouths
   for doors,
dark and cavernous,
dangerous in that way only strangers are.

The sun came in never-ending and yellow,
clouds hung like bedsheets in oranges and blues.
Our arms were never too far from our mother,
we had to protect her from the monsters under
     the bed.

We whispered in each other's ears
and lit the necessary fire in our bellies.
We spoke as if the sun would never rise again.
We spoke with laughter dripping from our lips,
trying to be braver,
and decided we would save the world.
With sticks as our swords
and sharpened ends
we saved the day
again.

JAY HULME

illustrations by Joe Manners

Community

The street I grew up on
was closed doors, closed lips and padlocks.
Our neighbours didn't have a spare key,
or the alarm code.
We were told somebody started
a Neighbourhood Watch,
but I never met anyone
I knew for sure was a neighbour.
We were all just figures, behind net curtains.

In the winters I'd walk the dog round the block,
hood up, head down, letting the world pass me by.
But as the sun left the sky
I'd look through windows
when I knew no one could see me.
The guy at Number Three loved the air force,
and the old man at Seven didn't own a TV.
He just sat there reading, silently.
Fourteen kept the curtains closed,
Fifteen didn't own any curtains.

The woman at Twenty-one watched VHS tapes of
   Countdown
even years after VHS died.
Thirty-six had seven cats,
Thirty-eight was always ironing,
and Forty-two spent all their time together, as a
   family.

It's amazing what you see,
looking in from the dark.
You see a myriad of people
and in every one, a heart.
A fully formed community
just waiting to start.

How Brave We Are

I was on the bus,
The clouds parted,
The sun became
A rainbow,
And I thought:

How brave we are,
To chase the dreams
That lie
At the end
Of such light.

I Thought I Was Small

I thought I was small
when I first went to London
and looked up at the skyscrapers,
and every one
cast an infinite shadow.

When I moved to a new city
and everyone was busy,
and the people I met
didn't know my first name,
and I didn't bother to tell them.
When I didn't notice
that everything I did
cast a shadow just as tall
as all of the skyscrapers
in London.

When I didn't notice the heart
built into my body.
When I didn't notice the universe
held within my soul.
I thought I was small.

New Words

I was meant to write a poem,
But the words just ran away,
They settled into lines at night
But ran at break of day.
Perhaps they went to Paris,
Or maybe to Peru,
I heard word of words in India
And even Timbuktu.

I searched for them in every place,
I travelled half the world,
And when I came back home again
I found some new words curled
On my tongue and in my pockets,
Letters latched upon my hair.
I could speak in languages
I didn't know were there.

So though I lost the words
I formed so carefully,
I found a thousand languages
That lie across the sea.
I can speak to many people
With these words that I have found
And discovered that the world's not flat,
It's very, very round.

Reflect It Back

Temples welcome you in,
Absorb your silence,
And reflect it back.

Churches welcome you in,
Absorb your silence,
And reflect it back.

Mosques welcome you in,
Absorb your silence,
And reflect it back.

Synagogues welcome you in,
Absorb your silence,
And reflect it back.

As life welcomes you in,
Absorbs your silence,
And reflects it back.

Sunset at Brean Down

We walked on the shoreline,
My old dog and me,
Our feet being rushed
By the rippling sea.

The tide swept in
To the rock and the cliff,
And we stood there in silence,
Taking in this:

The stillness of movement
As waves overlap,
They keep coming forwards
But always go back,

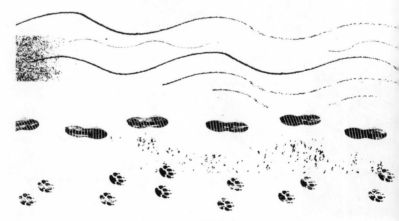

The pawprints and boot-marks
Both washing away,
The tide comes in closer
And pulls at the day.

We're stretching in sunlight,
Our shadows on sand,
They crawl up the cliffs
Like they're clinging to land,

And as sun touches water
And drowns in the sea,
We watch from the shoreline,
My old dog and me.

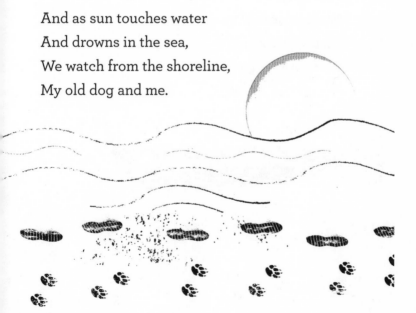

Peas

Being normal is boring.
It's like the sky when it's grey out,
or the fourth slice of plain toast,
or peas (unless you hate peas,
then it's not like peas at all).
Because normal isn't bad,
it's just normal,
it's just ordinary.
And no one on Earth
is ordinary.
No one on Earth
is peas.

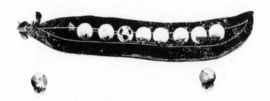

This Border

I walked through history.
The ghosts walked with me,
I could feel them beneath my feet.
They stood together, reaching gently
across this border where we meet.

I wished they'd teach me
what stands before me,
what types of mystery lie ahead.
But they stay silent. I forgive the
secrets guarded by the dead.

AMINA JAMA

Illustrations by Elanor Chuah

City

There's a group of school children flying home.
There's a man swinging his walking aid
as he gallops down the high street.
There's a preacher shuffling bibles
like a magic trick
as a choir assembles behind him.
There's an angel floating on the train.
There are synchronised swimmers in
a flooded bathroom.
There's a camel handing me change
as a cashier in Sainsbury's.
There's a flood of people walking
towards Paddington Station.
There are 24-hour happiness drive-throughs.
There's the sun setting on each day.

Pray

When your shadow gets up
and abandons you in your sleep,
may you envelope your
beginning and leave it on the coast.
May you let the day in
through your window.
May you give away your key.
May your teeth forget
the feeling of chattering.
May you open up your chest
and let the winter out.
May the glass in you never shatter.
May your words stop
letting you down.
May you laugh without thinking.
May you eat spaghetti with sugar
and fly to the moon.

May you let me in.

Dos

We sat in pairs in the garden at the start of summer,
the sun hitting our twin closed eyelids,
doubling our thoughts to a hew of orange.
Good weather is never a duet, never lasts
    for very long.

When rain falls, it rhymes
in couplets; there are always
two milk bottles open.

Recurring Dream

As a child
I would have
the same dream.
A balloon following
me around the
house. My family
sitting talking loudly.
Not seeing me
hiding
in a pink box.
Me running,
tripping, turning
to find the
balloon hanging
from my curtain
rail like melted
wax.

The House at the End of the Street

There were worn old mattresses outside
and broken beds and TVs left to die.

There were officers and firemen going in and out
as the whole street heard cries, screams and shouts.

There were stacks of books when you walked
    through
and all the walls were white with a hint of blue.

There were suitcases packed and left at the door
and enough tears to make a seashore.

There was a distant burnt smell
and everyone tiptoed as if on egg shells.

There was a smoke cloud of anger and pain
and Leila just stared at the light.

She stood with her back to it all,
I could see she was fighting the urge to crawl
    into a ball.

Leila was my best friend since Year Two.
For years we got each other through.

I was there when her dad left her mum,
I plaited her hair and stroked her heart until she
    was numb.

Now she was moving out from the house at the end
    of the street
and another kid would come into class and take
    her seat.

When Leila turned to me, I looked at her eyes.
They screamed that this was not goodbye.

Spring

Lost leaves at winter
find their way back home like a
dormant Lego piece.

Car Ride

Every summer on road trips with my dad,
he always played the same songs,
but he could never remember the right words.

He would sing, 'The Grand Old Duke of Pork...'
"No, Dad!" we'd scream. "It's York!"

No matter how many times we'd tell him
that there was no Twinkle, Twinkle, Little Fart,
and the song was not Row, Row, Row Your Goat,

he'd never remember for the next road trip.

My Cousin's Clothes

always consist of blue,
blue mornings,
blue feelings,
blue jeans.

She always kept her uniform
folded, never hung,
wore trousers, not skirts.
My brother called her an icon,

screamed I should be more like her
and not draw attention
to this body of bones
God left at my Moses basket.

My mother said I was more girl,
laughed how my cousin would
grow to be a firefighter
and I would be loved by one instead.

But they were both wrong.

She wore blue better
than a sunset wore orange,
never walked in anyone's shadow
but led every march.

She was more confident,
lively, vibrant,
brave, warm,
than I ever was.

Ruth Awolola is a student, youth worker and poet currently based in south-east London. Born in 1998, she has been writing since 2015 and in that year she was a winner of SLAMbassadors. At the moment in her poetry she is enjoying exploring themes of family, race, travelling and space. She hopes to go on to study English Literature and Education, with the intention of becoming a full-time educator.

Victoria Adukwei Bulley is a
British-Ghanaian poet, writer and filmmaker, born
in 1991. A former Barbican Young Poet, her work
has been commissioned by the Royal Academy of
Arts, and has also featured on BBC Radio 4.
Her debut pamphlet, *Girl B*, edited by Kwame
Dawes, is part of the 2017 New-Generation African
Poets series. Victoria is the director of
MOTHER TONGUES, an intergenerational poetry,
film and translation project supported by
Arts Council England and Autograph ABP.
She lives in London.

Abigail Cook is a performance poet
from London. Born in 1997, she is a 2015
SLAMbassadors winner and has performed at
the Southbank Centre. She is currently studying
Performance and Creative Enterprise,
which is in its second year, with a
discipline in spoken word, under a scholarship
at Guildhall School of Music and Drama.

Jay Hulme is a Transgender performance poet
from Leicester. Born in 1997, he's a winner
of SLAMbassadors 2015, and a finalist
in the 2016 Roundhouse slam.
He has self-published two solo collections
and been featured in anthologies.
Now residing in Bristol, he spends his time
writing and performing.

Amina Jama is a Somali-British writer
and is Roundhouse/BBC Radio 1Xtra's Words First
London finalist. Born in 1997, Amina was raised in
Bow, east London and is a member of collectives
Octavia and Barbican Young Poets. Amina's work
has been published in a Saqi Books anthology,
The Things I Would Tell You. It has been said that
her work is brave and humble with a warm intimacy,
both on stage and on the page.

About the Illustrators

Riya Chowdhury is an illustrator from Birmingham who works in a varied range of mediums. She usually works traditionally but also enjoys digital methods. Experimentation with art is something she believes to be important as new experiences can be developed into new techniques. She is happy to work with different genres but particularly enjoys illustrating science fiction and fantasy.

Elanor Chuah is a Malaysian illustrator whose work centres round narrative and editorial illustrations. One of her main influences is Japanese media, as she grew up looking at Japanese cartoons and comics. Aside from her childhood, other artists, movies and games are a huge influence on her work. Elanor trained as a concept/pre-production artist for three years, which makes working digitally her comfort zone. When she isn't drawing, you can find her cooking food from different cuisines and cultures.

Joe Manners is a freelance illustrator currently based in Birmingham, UK. He is inspired by genres surrounding dystopia, and by science fiction. His work is largely focused in the editorial sector, but he enjoys exploring a range of different areas.

★

The illustrators of *Rising Stars* all studied Illustration at Birmingham City University.

About Pop Up Projects

Pop Up is a non-profit social enterprise delivering imaginative and far-reaching children's literature programmes across the UK and internationally, often in deprived and challenged communities. They mainly create literature festivals in primary, secondary and special schools, as well as museums and libraries, through their flagship national Pop Up Festival. They also produce talent and professional development opportunities for writers and illustrators. The *Rising Stars* collaboration with Otter-Barry Books is one of a number of initiatives which seek out, nurture and support diverse aspiring and emerging literary talent to create literature, access the children's publishing industry and reach new readers. You can find out more about Pop Up at www.pop-up.org.uk – you can also explore their unique platform for young readers in schools: www.pop-up-hub.com.